BRANCH

and the Cooking Catastrophe

*For my parents, who bought me books
and read them to me*

 Published in the United States by Random House Children's Books, a division of Penguin Random House LLC, 1745 Broadway, New York, NY 10019, and in Canada by Penguin Random House Canada Limited, Toronto, in conjunction with DreamWorks Animation LLC. Random House and the colophon are registered trademarks of Penguin Random House LLC.

randomhousekids.com

ISBN 978-1-5247-1708-7 (trade) — ISBN 978-1-5247-1709-4 (lib. bdg.)
ISBN 978-1-5247-1710-0 (ebook)

Printed in the United States of America

10 9 8 7 6 5 4 3 2 1

DreamWorks

Trolls

BRANCH

and the Cooking Catastrophe

By David Lewman

Random House 🏠 New York

CHAPTER ONE

Deep in his highly camouflaged, heavily fortified, Bergen-proof survival bunker, Branch sat in a comfortable old chair made of tree bark and acorn caps. The Troll's blue hair stood straight up from his head, as it always did, and his big bare feet were propped up on a mushroom footstool.

He was sipping hot spiced tea and thinking.

Maybe it was time for a change to his home. Though he loved his bunker, its purpose had been lost the moment Queen Poppy brought the Trolls and the Bergens together in friendship. The whole point of living underground in a survival bunker was to hide from the Bergens. Now Branch didn't have to hide anymore. At least, not from Bergens.

He didn't want to move into one of the colorful, fuzzy pods that hung from the branches of the trees in Troll Village. That just wasn't his style. No, Branch planned on staying underground. He liked it there. He liked the dim light and the smell of the cool soil. He'd even made friends with a couple of worms who'd passed through a few times. Not *close* friends, but friends.

Maybe he could make a *few* changes. Add a skylight to let in a little sunshine now and then. A patio to enjoy on a nice day. And he'd always wanted a hot tub to soak in!

Branch smiled. *Yes,* he thought, *I have to admit that things are looking up around here, now that we don't have to worry about the Bergens.*

KNOCK! KNOCK! KNOCK! KNOCK!

Branch was startled out of his pleasant thoughts. Someone was pounding on his front door up on ground level! He got out of his cozy chair and hurried over to his periscope. Peering into the eyepiece, he saw Cooper standing on his stoop. The striped, giraffelike Troll was holding an envelope. "Be right there, Cooper!" Branch shouted into a speaking tube.

Up above, Cooper was startled to hear his friend's voice. "Where are you, Branch? I hear you, but I don't see you! Have you found a way to make yourself . . . INVISIBLE?" Cooper swung his head around, looking in every direction. Twists of blue hair flipped from side to side beneath his green hat.

Branch opened the secret door beneath the mat that lay on top of his bunker. "Yes, Cooper?" he asked. "What is it?"

"What's what?" Cooper asked, confused. "You mean that thing you just opened? A door! Yay, I love riddles! Ask me another!"

"I mean," Branch said, getting a little frustrated, "what did you come to see me about?"

"Oh!" Cooper said. "I brought you this!

From Queen Poppy!" He handed Branch the envelope.

"From Poppy?" Branch asked, excited. He looked at it. Like all envelopes from Poppy, it was decorated with lots of stickers, felt, and glitter. The front was addressed TO BRANCH—URGENT!

He tore it open, and a little drawing of Poppy popped up. A tiny voice said, "Branch! Come quickly! Hurry!" *POOF!* A cloud of glitter sprayed Branch's face.

"Poppy needs me!" Branch cried, brushing glitter off his nose. "Thanks, Cooper! See you later!" He rushed off toward Troll Village with the sparkly message.

"No problem!" Cooper called after him. "Maybe next time you can ask me more riddles!"

When Branch got to Poppy's pod, he ran inside without knocking. "Poppy!" he gasped, breathing hard. "What is it? What's the emergency? Are you in danger? Are we ALL in danger?"

Poppy looked up from a scrapbook she was working on and smiled. "Hey, Branch! Thanks for coming over so fast!"

"Well," Branch said, holding up the card, "your message says 'Come quickly!' So I figured it was really important."

Poppy stood up and brushed scrapbooking materials off her dress. "Oh, it is! I have a terrific idea!"

Branch frowned. He'd run all the way to Poppy's pod just so she could tell him about her terrific idea?

"Okaaay," he said slowly. "What's your idea?"

"A party!" Poppy announced.

"A party?" Branch repeated. "That's ALWAYS your idea!"

"But not just any party," she explained. "I think we should throw a great big picnic to celebrate our new friendship with the Bergens. Brilliant, huh?"

"A picnic with the Bergens?" Branch asked. He wasn't convinced that Poppy's terrific idea was all that terrific. "Why a picnic?"

"The Bergens are too big to fit inside even our biggest pod, so we should get together with them outdoors. A picnic is perfect!"

Branch guessed that made sense. But he still wasn't convinced.

"Look," Poppy said, picking up her scrapbook. "Here's what I have in mind." Turning the pages, she showed Branch her plan for the picnic. One page showed the Trolls inviting the Bergens. The Bergens looked thrilled. The next page showed Trolls and Bergens preparing a feast.

On the following page, they worked together to arrange the perfect spot in a clearing. Another page showed Trolls and Bergens arriving with the food. The next-to-last page of the scrapbook pictured Trolls and Bergens spending a sunny day happily eating together. And the last page showed the night of the picnic, with everyone oohing and aahing at big beautiful bursts of glitter that lit up the starry sky.

"Pretty nice, huh?" Poppy said.

"Sure," Branch agreed. "It looks great—in scrapbook form. In reality, I have no idea how it'll turn out."

"In reality," Poppy predicted confidently, "it'll be even greater!"

"What are you going to call this picnic of yours?" Branch asked.

Poppy squinched up her face, considering. "Hmm," she said. "I hadn't thought about that. Any suggestions?"

"Disaster Day?" Branch suggested. "Catastro-fest? Mess-o-palooza?"

Poppy gently threw a wadded-up ball of felt at Branch. "Why are you being so negative? You've been so positive since we became friends with the Bergens!"

"Sorry," Branch said, picking up the felt ball

and tossing it in the air. "Force of habit. I'm just not sure this picnic of yours is going to be easy. No one's ever invited Trolls and Bergens to the same party before."

"That's what makes it so exciting!" Poppy said, throwing her arms open wide. "It's brand-new! We'll be breaking ground in picnicking! We'll be explorers! Discoverers! Pioneers!"

"Don't explorers and pioneers often end up starving to death? Or getting lost in the snow?" asked Branch.

Poppy couldn't believe what she was hearing. "It's summer!" she exclaimed. "There isn't going to be any snow. And it's a picnic, so no one's going to starve to death."

Branch plopped down onto one of Poppy's colorful cushions. "Okay, okay. No one's going to starve. And there won't be snow. But let me ask you something."

"Sure, Branch," Poppy said cheerfully, flopping onto another cushion. "Anything! Ask away!"

"Why are you telling *me* all this?" he asked. "Why was it so urgent and important that I run over here to learn about your plans?"

Poppy grinned, leaned back, and put her hands behind her head. "Ah," she said. "Good question. I want you to go up to the castle in Bergen Town and work with King Gristle on the menu."

Branch stared at her, stunned. Then he jumped up and shouted, "Me? Work with King Gristle on planning a picnic? All he likes to eat are *Trolls*!"

"Gristle never actually ate a Troll, remember? And the Bergens' Troll-eating days are *over*," Poppy said gently. "You've been to the castle, and you've met King Gristle, so he already knows you. You're the perfect one to work with him. This whole picnic is about Trolls and Bergens coming together! Will you do it? For me? Please?"

Branch hesitated. He really wasn't sure about working with King Gristle on anything, let alone a picnic. But he couldn't let Poppy down.

"Okay, I'll do it," he said.

Poppy threw her arms around Branch. "Thank you, Branch! You're the best! And this is going to be the greatest Troll-Bergen picnic ever!"

"Well, it's also going to be the *first* Troll-Bergen picnic ever, so there isn't a whole lot of competition," Branch said. "I'll go talk to Gristle, but I'm not making any promises. He may think this is a *terrible* idea!"

CHAPTER TWO

"That's a TERRIFIC idea!" King Gristle exclaimed in the castle's throne room, clapping enthusiastically. "I LOVE picnics!"

He jumped off his throne, almost landing on the tail of his pet alligator, Barnabus. The king's green hair was neatly combed, and he wore blue shorts, a red-and-white-striped shirt, a fur-lined cape, a gold crown, and sandals with socks.

"You *do*?" Branch said, surprised by the Bergen's gusto.

"Sure!" King Gristle said, sitting back down on his throne. "I mean, I've never actually been to one, but I've heard about them, and they sound WONDERFUL!" He leaned over to pet Barnabus, who was hiding under the throne. As he scratched the alligator's long snout fondly, Barnabus made low growls of contentment deep in his throat. *Rrrrnnrrrrh . . .*

Branch nodded, taking it all in. *So I'm going to be planning a picnic with someone who's never been to one,* he thought. "Okay," he said. "Great! Well, Queen Poppy wants us to work on the menu together."

Gristle stopped petting Barnabus. He looked up and frowned. "Oh. That might be a problem.

You see, I'm not much of a cook. As in, I've never cooked anything. Ever. Eating, I'm very good at. But cooking, not so much."

Branch scrambled up the throne and stood on one of its arms so he could look Gristle in the eye. "That's okay. You don't have to do the cooking. You and I will just plan it out. You know, pick the recipes. Make sure we have all the equipment we need. Gather the ingredients. Other Bergens and Trolls will do the actual cooking."

King Gristle got off his throne again and paced back and forth as Barnabus watched, his head swinging from side to side. "I see," Gristle said. "That makes sense. But where will we find these recipes?"

"Um, in your kitchen?" Branch suggested.

"I have a kitchen?" Gristle said. "I mean . . . to the Royal Kitchen!"

He hurried out of the throne room, and Branch ran after him. Meanwhile, Barnabus curled up and went to sleep, dreaming of cool streams and tasty fish.

ℓℓℓℓℓℓℓℓ

The Royal Kitchen had seen better days. In fact, it was a terrible mess, with dirty pots and pans stacked from floor to ceiling. The room looked as though it hadn't been cleaned in weeks, if not months. It didn't smell great, either.

"Sorry about the mess," King Gristle said sheepishly. "Ever since Chef . . . left . . ."

Branch nodded. He'd been there the night Chef was thrown out of the castle. The evil, power-mad cook hadn't been seen since. It was rumored that she now lived somewhere deep in the forest with Creek, a Troll who had been thrown out of the castle along with her, and used his hair to scrub her dishes.

"Who's in charge of your meals now?" Branch asked.

Gristle shrugged, a little embarrassed. "Mostly we order delivery. Lots of pizza." Then his face brightened. "Hey, maybe we could have pizza at the picnic!"

Branch wasn't sure. He thought about the picnics he'd been to, and he didn't remember pizza ever being served. "Where did Chef keep her recipes?" he asked.

Gristle's small eyes opened wide, and he raised his hands, perplexed. "I have no idea!"

"Okay," Branch sighed. "Then we'll have to look for them."

The Troll and the Bergen began to search the Royal Kitchen together. It was a *big* kitchen, with lots of grimy wooden cabinets and shelves. Branch looked low and Gristle looked high.

Branch opened a drawer close to the floor. *FLOOMPF!* A furry creature jumped out and scrambled across the kitchen! The force of it knocked the Troll to the floor.

While rifling through a cabinet near the ceiling, King Gristle looked down at Branch. "What happened?" he said. "Did you slip? I should've warned you—the floor's really greasy."

"You've got wild animals living in this kitchen," Branch announced. "Pretty sure that was a striped furmunk. They have big families. Where there's one, there are sure to be more."

"Really?" Gristle said, excited. "Cool! I've always wanted to see one of those!"

"Find any recipes yet?" Branch asked, picking himself up and opening another drawer cautiously.

King Gristle shook his head. "Not yet. So far all I've found are those round things for cooking food in."

"Pots and pans?" Branch asked.

"I guess," Gristle said. "If you say so."

Branch managed to keep from rolling his eyes, but he thought, *How am I supposed to plan a picnic with someone who doesn't know what pots and pans are called?*

They searched for a while without talking.

The only sounds were the clatters and clanks of pans and utensils. Branch couldn't find a single recipe. He began to think maybe Chef had taken them all with her.

But then King Gristle called, "I think I found something! Look at this!"

Branch closed a drawer full of battered spoons and forks and hurried across the floor to join the young king.

In a dark corner of the big kitchen, a tall, narrow door stretched to the ceiling. A sign on the door said CHEF'S SECRET RECIPE CLOSET! KEEP OUT OR YOU'LL BE SORRY! I MEAN IT! SIGNED, CHEF. PS: *I REALLY MEAN IT!*

"That's great!" Branch said. "She must have kept her recipes in this closet!"

"Yeah," Gristle said, "but we can't go in there."

Branch snorted. "Why not?"

"Because it says right on the sign that we'll be sorry!" The king pointed at the door. "And she really means it!"

"Look around," Branch said calmly. "Do you see Chef anywhere?"

Gristle looked. "No," he admitted. "But she could be hiding! Like that striped furmunk was!"

Branch sighed. "Chef is a lot bigger than a striped furmunk. She isn't hiding in one of these drawers. She isn't anywhere *near* this castle. Or Bergen Town, for that matter."

"How do you know?" Gristle asked suspiciously.

"Because you banished her!" Branch said. "And when King Gristle banishes Bergens, they stay banished! Right?"

Gristle stood a little taller. "That's right!"

"So there's NO WAY Chef is hiding in this kitchen!"

"RIGHT!"

"Now let's OPEN THIS SECRET RECIPE CLOSET!"

"YEAH!"

Gristle flung open the door. *ZWIT! ZWIT! ZWIT!* Arrows shot out of the closet, knocking off his crown and pinning it to the wall! The king and Branch hit the deck.

"Of course," Branch admitted from his spot on the greasy floor, "the closet could be booby-trapped."

"You think?" Gristle said sarcastically, carefully reaching up to retrieve his crown.

They slowly crawled toward the open door. Inside the small, gloomy closet, they could see the outlines of a cabinet with drawers.

"The recipes must be in that cabinet," Branch whispered. He didn't want to set off any more traps.

"Should we open it?" Gristle whispered back nervously.

"We've got to," Branch said determinedly. "But we'd better be careful."

"Right!" the king agreed. "Um . . . how?"

Branch dug through drawers and cabinets, searching for utensils with long handles. He dragged them out and piled them up. Then he found a big spool of twine and tied them together, making one long tool that stretched all the way across the kitchen.

"We'll use this to open the cabinet," he said. "That way if there's a booby trap, at least we won't be standing right in front of it."

"Brilliant!" Gristle said. "I like your plan!"

"Since you're bigger, you should do it," added Branch.

"I don't like that part," the young king complained. But he picked up the makeshift tool and carefully guided it toward the cabinet, edging the doors open. Branch had tied a loop on the end of the tool to slip around the drawer handles.

CLINK!

Gristle caught the loop on the handle of the bottom drawer. "Got it!" he cried.

"Good!" Branch said. "Now pull the drawer open . . . slowly."

King Gristle eased his big green hands along the tool and pulled, easing the drawer open, until . . . *WHOP!*

CHEF POPPED OUT!

CHAPTER THREE

"AAAAHHHH!" Gristle screamed. "CHEF! SHE'S BACK!" He dove behind a table, his knees knocking together.

Branch peered at Chef. At first he'd been startled to see the nasty Bergen pop out of the cabinet drawer. But as he examined her (from across the kitchen), he saw that she wasn't moving. She was just sticking out of the drawer, holding her hands up in a menacing position.

He carefully approached the closet. He picked up a cork from the floor and threw it at Chef. *BONK!* The cork bounced off her. She swayed a little, but her face stayed exactly the same, and she didn't say anything.

"That's not Chef," Branch said, walking confidently into the closet. "That's just a *cardboard cutout* of Chef! She probably thought it would scare us."

"She was right," Gristle muttered, wiping sweat off his brow.

Together they pulled the cutout from the cabinet and tossed it aside. Then they started looking through the recipes. They were written on little cards, most of them yellowed with age and spattered with ingredients. Many of the recipes were for preparing . . . Trolls!

"There must be *hundreds* of recipes in here," Branch said, shuddering as he flipped through the cards. "I had no idea Bergens ate so many different dishes. How are we going to decide which ones to make for the picnic?"

Gristle carefully pulled open another drawer. Nothing popped out. He started flipping through the recipe cards there while Branch continued to look at the ones in the bottom drawer. "The key to a good picnic," Gristle said, "is having plenty of savory dishes. In Bergen Town, savory rules—the saltier, the better!" He licked his lips just thinking about it.

"I thought you said you've never *been* to a picnic," Branch said.

"Maybe not," Gristle admitted. "But I've

been to lots of Bergen feasts, and the food is always super savory, with plenty of salt."

"Okay," Branch said, "but when you're fixing food for Trolls, you can't beat something sweet. The sweets—especially the cupcakes—make the picnic. Or feast. Or meal. Or snack." He was getting hungry.

Gristle looked doubtful. Then he pulled a sealed brown envelope out of the cabinet. It was labeled TOP-SECRET!

"What's this?" he said. "Should we open it?"

"Of course we should open it," Branch answered.

"But it says 'Top-Secret!'" Gristle pointed out, hesitating. "I thought you weren't supposed to open top-secret documents."

"And *I* thought you were the king around

here, which means you can open any envelope in the castle if you want to!" Branch said.

"You're right! I *am* the king! It's envelope-openin' time!" Gristle said, ripping it open. He squeezed the sides together so he could see inside, making sure it wasn't booby-trapped. Then he reached in and pulled out a card. As he read it, his reddish-brown eyes widened. "Do you know what this is?" His voice trembled a little.

"A recipe?" Branch guessed.

"Yes," Gristle said, "but not just *any* recipe! This is Chef's famous and super-secret *pizza* recipe! We could make this for the picnic!"

Branch still wasn't sure about having pizza at a picnic. For Trolls, it was all about the sweets. He decided maybe he'd done enough work with King Gristle for one day.

"A famous super-secret recipe!" he said, trying to sound positive, like Poppy. "That's great! Why don't you start figuring out how to get a bunch of the best Bergen dishes made for the picnic? Meanwhile, I'll head back to Troll Village and get everyone there working on the sweets."

Gristle made a face. "Okay, but not *too* many sweets." He patted his bulging tummy. "I'm kinda on a diet."

When Branch got to Troll Village, he headed straight to the bakery. Inside, Biggie and several other Trolls were making lots of sweets. DJ Suki and her Wooferbug were providing lively music to cook by.

"Hello, Branch!" Biggie called over the pounding rhythm when he saw his friend come in. "Poppy told us all about the big picnic! So we're baking lots and lots of delicious sweets. Like I always say, you can't beat something sweet!"

Branch nodded and grinned. The bakery smelled wonderful. Cupcakes were stacked up high. Beaters were spinning in the mixers, making up batches of batter. The ovens were hot, baking all sorts of desserts to a beautiful golden brown. There was plenty of frosting ready to decorate the treats once they cooled. Branch inhaled deeply through his nose, savoring the marvelous scents.

"We'll need lots of sweets, Biggie," Branch said. "Bergens are hungry. And big!"

"I know," Biggie agreed. "That's why I've been experimenting with some larger items. Take a look at these cookies."

The big blue Troll led Branch to a platter of enormous cookies shaped like his pet worm, Mr. Dinkles. They were even the same size as him!

"I had Mr. Dinkles model for these," Biggie said proudly, "and he did a really good job! Of course, he's had a lot of practice modeling for pictures."

Biggie gestured toward a wall covered in photos of Mr. Dinkles dressed up in different costumes: a flower, a dragon, a unicorn . . .

"Very nice," Branch said, admiring the worm-shaped cookies. "By the way, where *is* Mr. Dinkles?"

"Well, he's right . . ." Biggie looked around and started to panic. "That's funny. He was here a minute ago. Mr. Dinkles? Where are you? MR. DINKLES!"

The worm popped up from the pile of cookies that looked exactly like him. "Mew!" he said. Then he chewed a mouthful of cookie. *CRUNCH! CRUNCH! CRUNCH!*

Biggie picked up his pet and hugged him. "Mr. Dinkles! There you are! Good boy!"

Branch looked at one of the Mr. Dinkles cookies. "These are great, but are you sure they're big enough? I mean, to us, this is a really big cookie. But to a Bergen, it's about the size of a button."

Biggie nodded. "You're right. I thought of that. Check *these* out!" He showed Branch another platter of cookies. They were even bigger than the Mr. Dinkles cookies, and they were shaped like Trolls. In fact, they looked almost exactly like Branch. Life-sized Branch cookies!

"You like them?" Biggie asked eagerly.

"They're . . . impressive," Branch said, not wanting to hurt the sensitive Troll's feelings. Biggie could cry at the drop of a cupcake. "I mean, how you managed to make such big cookies without them breaking or cracking— it's pretty amazing."

"Some cookies in the first batch broke," Biggie admitted. "We already ate those."

BURP! Mr. Dinkles belched loudly.

"But . . . ," Branch began.

"Yes?" Biggie asked anxiously.

"I'm just not sure it's such a good idea, making cookies in the shape of Trolls," Branch explained. "I mean, we don't want to remind the Bergens of how much they enjoyed eating us."

Biggie nodded slowly. "You're right. I never thought of that." He looked disappointed for a moment, remembering how much time he'd put into making the big Troll cookies. Branch was afraid he was going to cry. But then Biggie brightened. "I guess we'll just have to eat them ourselves!"

He picked up a Branch cookie. *CRUNCH!* Biggie bit off an ear. Branch flinched as Biggie munched happily.

"So maybe you could make some more big cookies," Branch suggested "Just not, you know, in the shape of Trolls."

With his mouth full and crumbs dropping onto his chest, Biggie nodded. "Come on! Let me show you the rest of the sweets we're making!"

Biggie led the way through the bakery. He showed Branch the cookies, cupcakes, rolls, pies, doughnuts, eclairs, cream puffs, brownies, tarts, layer cakes, and turnovers they were preparing for the big picnic.

Guy Diamond stood over a bunch of baked cupcakes, dancing to DJ Suki's music. Every time he shook his body, glitter rained down onto the pastries.

"If Guy's going to work in the bakery, maybe he should at least wear an apron," Branch said, frowning. "And is that glitter edible?"

Biggie popped one of the shiny cupcakes

into his mouth, chewed, swallowed, and gave a big thumbs-up. "Yup!" he announced. "Totally edible!"

Meanwhile, back at the castle, Gristle was working on his part of the preparations. . . .

CHAPTER FOUR

KNOCK! KNOCK! KNOCK!

King Gristle tapped on the door to Bridget's room. "Hello?" he called. "Anybody home? Bridget?"

The door swung open and Bridget stood there with a toothy grin. "Hi, Gristle! I mean, Your Majesty! I mean, Your Royal Bergenness!" She tried to smooth her apron as she nervously shifted from foot to foot. Though the apron was wrinkled and stained, her light-blue skin was freshly scrubbed, and she wore her pink hair in neat pigtails.

"Hi, Lady Glittersparkles! I mean, Bridget!" he answered. "It's okay to call me Gristle, by the way."

"Okay . . . Gristle," Bridget said shyly. "You can call me Bridget."

"I just did."

"Oh, yeah."

They stood there for a moment, staring into each other's little eyes.

"Was there . . . something you wanted?" Bridget prompted.

"Huh?" Gristle said, snapping to attention. "Oh, yes! There *was* something I wanted: help!"

Bridget looked surprised and concerned. "You need help? From me? Did you hurt yourself? Are you in danger? Is someone chasing you?" She looked past him down the hall to see if any monsters were after him.

"I don't think so," Gristle said, checking over his shoulder to make sure. "No—what I need help with is food for a picnic!"

"Picnic?" Bridget asked, puzzled. She'd never heard of a Bergen king going on a picnic.

Gristle explained about the big picnic with the Bergens and the Trolls. He said he and Branch were organizing the food, but he could use Bridget's help. "I mean, since you used to work with Chef in the Royal Kitchen."

"I was just the scullery maid," Bridget said, "cleaning up pots and pans. Other Bergens usually helped Chef with all the cooking."

Gristle hesitated. He didn't want to work with other Bergens. He wanted to work with Bridget. He was in love with her.

"They're all . . . busy," he lied. "Come on." He quickly took her hand. "Let's go to the Royal Kitchen and figure out what we'll need."

As he led her down the hallway, Bridget looked at their clasped hands and smiled. She dared to give Gristle's hand a little squeeze, and he squeezed back.

The Royal Kitchen was still a terrible mess, with dirty dishes stacked high. "Sorry I haven't cleaned this up," Bridget said. "But since Chef . . . left . . . there was no one in charge to tell me what to do."

That was a bit of a fib. Bridget *knew* the

dishes needed cleaning; she just didn't want to do it. She hated washing dishes. So without Chef to boss her around, she'd stayed out of the kitchen completely.

"Oh, that's okay!" Gristle reassured her. "Don't worry about it!" He led her to the closet with the cabinet. "Branch and I found Chef's old recipes in here."

Bridget gasped. "Weren't you afraid of the booby traps? The arrows?" Then she noticed several arrows stuck in the kitchen wall opposite the closet.

Gristle waved his hand dismissively, as if he hadn't been scared at all. "Afraid? Me? Nah! It takes more than a few little arrows to scare *me*!" A striped furmunk scurried across the floor in front of them.

"AAAHHH!" Gristle shrieked.

"It's just a striped furmunk," Bridget explained, giggling softly. "It won't hurt you."

"Of course not," Gristle bristled, trying to regain some kingly dignity. "I was just worried that it might startle *you*."

"Thank you," Bridget said, smiling.

They started looking through the recipes together. Gristle showed Bridget the super-secret one he'd found for Chef's famous pizza. She whistled, impressed.

"Wow!" she said. "Pizza would be PERFECT for the big picnic!"

"That's exactly what I told Branch!" Gristle said, excited that Bridget agreed. "But I think we should have more than just pizza, don't you?"

"Definitely!"

"Wanna help me pick out the best recipes?"

"Sure!"

As they flipped through the old cards, Bridget helped choose recipes for the salty, savory dishes Bergens like best: pretzels, meat pies, sausages, chips, stuffed olives, pickled cabbage, and marinated turnips.

"YUM!" Gristle exclaimed. "This is going to be the most delicious picnic EVER!"

Bridget read Chef's pizza recipe. "Hmm," she said, frowning. "Some of the steps here— stacking the firewood in the oven, tossing the dough—seem kind of tricky."

Gristle leaned in to study the card. It was also a good excuse to get close to Bridget. "Maybe we need a pizza expert. Do we know one?"

The two Bergens thought a moment, then

smiled and said at the same time, "Captain Starfunkle!"

Captain Starfunkle ran the roller rink where Gristle and Bridget had gone on their first date. And his pizza was delicious!

"I say we go there right now!" Gristle said.

"Race ya! OnetwothreeGO!" Bridget yelled as she sprinted out of the kitchen.

The king smiled and ran after her. *What a girl!* he thought.

ℓℓℓℓℓℓℓℓℓ

At Captain Starfunkle's Roller Rink and Arcade, the owner read Chef's super-secret recipe. "Uh-huh . . . uh-huh," Captain Starfunkle murmured. When he looked up, his eyes were shining with happy tears. "Amazing. I've always wondered how Chef made her famous pizza. And now I know. I wonder, Your Majesty, may I ask you a favor?"

"Yes?" Gristle asked, his mouth full of the pizza Captain Starfunkle had generously given them free of charge.

"After this picnic, might Your Majesty grant me the right to serve Chef's famous pizza here at my roller rink?" He folded his hands and bowed while looking up at the king imploringly.

"Hmm," Gristle said, pretending to think about it. It was a trick his father had taught him. *"Son, when someone asks you a question, always act like you're thinking about it,"* the old king had advised. *"That way, you'll seem smart."* The truth was Gristle loved the idea of Captain Starfunkle serving Chef's delicious pizza. His pizza was good, but hers was *great.*

And now Gristle would be able to come and eat it any time he wanted to! And roller-skate! With Bridget! What could be better than that?

"I'll tell you what, Captain Starfunkle," Gristle finally said. "Help us make Chef's pizza for this picnic, and the recipe is yours. But don't call it Chef's pizza. We don't want people thinking too much about Chef and wishing she'd come back. She was bad news. Call it your pizza. Or maybe something like King Gristle's Fave-a-roo."

"Oh, thank you, Your Majesty!" Captain Starfunkle said, kissing the king's hand.

Gristle jerked his hand away. "That's enough hand-kissing! I don't like it! Spread the word!"

"Sorry, Your Majesty," Captain Starfunkle said.

"That's all right," Gristle said. "Do a good job on the pizza for this picnic and you just might become *Colonel* Starfunkle!" He winked.

Captain Starfunkle looked very pleased. He studied Chef's pizza recipe again. "How many diners will attend this picnic?"

"Well," Gristle said, "all the Bergens are invited."

"And all the Trolls," Bridget added between bites of pizza. "But they're small. They don't eat much."

Captain Starfunkle whistled. "*All* the Bergens? And all the Trolls? We're going to need a lot of pizza!"

"Sounds good to me!" Gristle enthused, picking up another slice. "What will you require?"

Captain Starfunkle scratched his warty chin,

thinking. "Several assistant chefs. Perhaps some of the cooks who served under Chef up at the castle."

Gristle nodded. "Fine, fine. What else?"

"Where will the picnic be held?" Captain Starfunkle asked.

"Somewhere near Troll Village, I believe," Gristle said. He looked around to make sure no Trolls were there to hear him. "You know, it takes them a lot longer to travel on those short legs. So we'll probably have the picnic near their place."

Captain Starfunkle shook his head and clucked his tongue. "Oh, dear," he sighed.

"What's the matter?" Bridget asked. "Don't you like Troll Village? They live in cute little pods! So colorful!"

"It's not that," he said. "It's just that pizza needs to be served hot, and by the time it travels all the way from Bergen Town to Troll Village, it'll be cold. Imagine—cold pizza!"

"Unacceptable!" Gristle cried, forgetting that he had often eaten cold pizza for breakfast and thoroughly enjoyed it. "What should we do?"

"I propose," Captain Starfunkle said, "that we construct special wood-burning pizza ovens near the site of the picnic. We can build them out of stone. What do you think, Your Majesty?"

"Excellent idea!" Gristle said, not bothering to pretend to think about the question. "I'll put out the word: we need stonemasons to build the new pizza ovens, and chefs to help cook the pizza!"

"And woodsmen to gather the exact kind of

firewood specified in Chef's recipe," Captain Starfunkle added.

"*Your* recipe," Gristle corrected him, and winked.

Captain Starfunkle grinned and nodded. "Yes, Your Majesty. *My* recipe."

"This is exciting!" Bridget said, clapping.

She wasn't the only one who thought so.

Soon word of the picnic was all over Bergen Town. The Bergens were excited at the thought of a big picnic with Chef's famous pizza, served hot from new wood-burning ovens. A few grumbled at the idea of eating food prepared by Trolls. "Won't there be hair in it?" several asked. But mostly, everyone couldn't wait for the picnic!

CHAPTER FIVE

Confident that everything was humming right along at the bakery, Branch headed back to Bergen Town to see how King Gristle was doing with the picnic preparations. As he entered the castle, Branch hoped things were going as smoothly for the Bergens as they were for the Trolls.

"Branch!" Gristle called out happily when

he spotted him striding into the throne room. "Good to see you again! How are things going in Troll Village? Making lots of savory treats for our big picnic?"

"Making lots of *sweet* treats," Branch said. "And it's all going very well. The ovens at the bakery are running day and night to meet the demand for all the pastries."

Gristle looked puzzled and a bit concerned. "Pastries, huh? That sounds . . . filling. By the way, are all your bakers wearing hairnets? There's been a little concern here in Bergen Town about Trolls getting hair into the food they make."

From the look on Branch's face, Gristle could tell he was offended.

"Not that your hair isn't very . . . *colorful*!"

Gristle said, trying to make things better. "It's just that we don't want to eat it. I mean, we *used* to want to eat it, but now . . . we don't. Not anymore."

Branch's eyes widened. He looked stunned.

Gristle sensed that he'd only made things worse. He raised his hands in apology. "Forget it," he said. "Forget about the hair. I'm sure your pastries will be . . . basically hair-free."

Taking a deep breath, Branch chose his words carefully. He was upset but didn't want to blow up at the king and ruin the picnic. "We Trolls," he began, "take very good care of our hair, including making sure it never gets into our food. Ever."

"That's excellent," Gristle said quickly, wishing he'd never brought up hair at all.

"How are *your* preparations coming along?" Branch asked.

King Gristle smiled proudly, happy to have the subject changed. "Very, very, very well!" He nodded, thinking about his trip to Captain Starfunkle's Roller Rink and Arcade with Bridget. After the pizza, they'd played arcade games for a couple of hours. Gristle had done particularly well at Whack-a-Troll, though he wasn't going to tell Branch that. In fact, he made a mental note to order Captain Starfunkle to change the game to something else. Whack-a-Striped-Furmunk? That didn't really have the same ring to it. . . .

Branch waited patiently for Gristle to tell him more. When he didn't, Branch asked, "What have you done, exactly?"

Gristle hopped down from his throne and walked around the room as he talked, gesturing enthusiastically with his hands. "First, I went into the dark, scary Royal Kitchen and found Chef's super-secret recipe for her famous pizza, even though it was in a booby-trapped cabinet!"

"I was there for that part," Branch said drily. "Remember?"

"Oh, right," Gristle said. "Then Bridget and I picked out a bunch more recipes." The king described all the savory delights the Bergens planned to cook for the picnic.

Branch managed to not make a face.

"We went to consult with Captain Starfunkle about the preparation of the pizza," Gristle continued. "He's a pizza expert." He excitedly told Branch about the plans to recruit Bergen chefs and stonemasons to build wood-burning pizza ovens near the picnic site. And to get woodsmen to gather the perfect firewood. He also told Branch how eager everyone in Bergen Town was about getting to eat Chef's famous pizza again.

"When the picnic is over, the stone pizza ovens will be our gift to the Trolls!" Gristle said, having just thought of the idea on the spot. He felt very pleased with himself for being so clever. "Free! No charge!"

Privately, Branch wondered what in the world the Trolls would do with giant stone ovens, but he nodded and said, "Thank you. Very generous of you."

"You're welcome!" Gristle said, grinning. "Maybe if this picnic is a success, we'll make it an annual event! We can use the pizza ovens every year!"

It seemed to Branch that Poppy's picnic was turning into a pizza party. He kept the thought to himself, though. "And what about the ingredients?" he asked.

"Ingredients?" Gristle echoed.

"Yes, ingredients," Branch said. "You know, the stuff you use to make the food."

Now it was Gristle's turn to look offended. "I *know* what ingredients are," he said stuffily.

"Great," Branch said. "Have you gotten them?"

"Well . . . no," Gristle admitted. "Not yet."

Branch was trying to keep his temper in check, but he snapped. "WHAT!" he shouted. "You haven't even gotten the ingredients yet?

We Trolls have already baked lots and lots of sweet pastries, and you Bergens haven't even gathered your ingredients? I *knew* this picnic would be a disaster!"

Gristle thought fast. He could see the little Troll was upset. The truth was Gristle had been so pleased with his trips to the Royal Kitchen and Captain Starfunkle's Roller Rink and Arcade that he'd forgotten all about getting ingredients.

But he wasn't about to admit that to Branch.

"Pastries are different," Gristle said. "You can make them ahead of time. But not pizza! It has to be fresh and hot! We can't make it until just before the picnic! So there's no rush about buying the ingredients! You see? Relax!"

Branch hated being told to relax. It reminded him of Creek, and he had never liked Creek. He hadn't been surprised when Creek turned out to be a traitor, betraying the other Trolls to save his own skin.

He took another deep breath. "May I suggest, King Gristle—"

"You can call me Gristle if you'd like."

"Gristle, I suggest that you and I gather all your recipes. We'll go through them and make a shopping list. Then we'll buy the ingredients."

"When?" Gristle asked.

"Right now!" Branch said impatiently. "It should have been done already!"

"Okay, okay," Gristle said, patting the air between them with his hands. "Let's do this!"

After a bit of searching, Gristle found the stack of recipe cards, a sheet of paper, and a pen. He and Branch put together a long shopping list. As Branch read the recipe for marinated turnips, he felt his stomach turn. *At least there'll be plenty of good sweets,* he thought.

When they'd finished making their list, Branch asked, "So where do we buy all this stuff?"

Gristle looked like he was pretending to think about Branch's question. But this time, he really *was* thinking about it. In his experience, either you ordered pizza from Captain Starfunkle's and they delivered it, or you went into the dining hall and ate the food that was already there. He had no idea where it came from.

"There are several possibilities," he said, stalling. "I suggest we . . . go ask Bridget."

They found Bridget in her room, reading a magazine. "Chef always got her ingredients from Grub Grubbington's Grocery Store. She said they were the best."

"Right!" Gristle said. "That's what I was thinking, too, but I just wanted to be sure the best place was still . . . what was it again?"

"Bridget said Grub Grubbington's Grocery Store," said Branch. "Sounds lovely?"

Actually, Grub Grubbington's Grocery Store *was* lovely, as Branch was surprised to see when they walked in. He also learned that when you go shopping with a king, you get excellent service. Grub Grubbington himself dashed about the store, filling their shopping cart with all the ingredients on their list.

Except for one . . .

CHAPTER SIX

"I am SO sorry, Your Most Excellent Majesty," Grub Grubbington said, wringing his hands, "but we seem to be all out of speckled savory salt!"

Gristle looked unconcerned. "That's all right, Grubbington. Don't worry about it! When will you be getting another shipment?"

Grub Grubbington consulted his calendar. "Let's see. Approximately . . . never."

"What!" Branch cried. "Never?"

"We haven't been able to stock speckled savory salt in a long time, sir," the anguished grocer explained. "It's very difficult to obtain."

Gristle took a container of salt from a shelf. "Maybe we can just use regular salt. Which recipe is the speckled savory salt for, anyway?"

Branch checked their list. "Chef's famous pizza."

Grub Grubbington and Gristle gasped.

"There can be no substitutions in *that* recipe!" Grubbington insisted. "To achieve the true delicious flavor, you will *have* to use genuine speckled savory salt! If you don't, any Bergen who has tasted Chef's famous pizza will *instantly* know the difference!"

"There could be protests! Riots! Looting!"

Gristle said, looking scared. "It could mean the end of my reign as king of the Bergens!"

"Really?" Branch asked. "Just because the pizza didn't taste right?"

"You obviously don't know Bergens," Gristle said.

Branch heaved a deep sigh. "Okay," he said, turning to Grub Grubbington. "You said this spotty salt stuff is difficult to obtain. Where would we go to get some?"

"Speckled savory salt can only be found in a crystal cave at the top of Mount Gloom. The cave is guarded by a fierce wing-dingle," Grubbington explained.

"Oooh, a wing-dingle!" Gristle squealed. "Just like the one on my Troll bi—" He stopped himself. He was about to say "Troll bib," but then realized Troll bibs—worn by Bergens when eating Trolls—were not the best thing to bring up around Branch. He started whistling a little tune, hoping to hide how awkward he felt.

"Wing-dingle," Branch scoffed. "That's just a myth! A bedtime story to scare little kids into being good!"

"It worked on me," Gristle muttered.

Grub Grubbington drew himself up to his full height and sniffed. "I assure you, sir, that the wing-dingle is real! It guards the crystal cave on Mount Gloom, and that is why *no one*—I repeat, *no one*—will be able to sell you speckled savory salt! When Chef made her famous pizza, she must have gone to the cave and braved the fierce wing-dingle herself!"

"I'll bet the wing-dingle was scared of *her*,"

Gristle said, putting on a positive face. "Well, there's nothing to be done. We'll just have to serve something besides Chef's famous pizza. Maybe we can double up on marinated turnips."

Branch looked doubtful. "But didn't you say all the Bergens were super excited about getting to eat this pizza of Chef's?"

Gristle shrugged. "Well, yes, but after years of being miserable, they're pretty used to disappointment."

"You said they'd riot if the pizza came out wrong!" said Branch.

"They're used to being miserable, but they're also very critical," said King Gristle. "And they like rioting."

Branch thought for a moment. He knew it was important to Poppy for the picnic to be a big success for the Trolls *and* the Bergens. And if that meant scaling Mount Gloom to get special salt, so be it.

"Gristle," he said, "it looks like you and I are going to climb a mountain."

The Bergen king turned pale green.

ℓℓℓℓℓℓℓℓℓ

After getting specific directions from the Royal Cartographer—the king called him the Royal Map Dude—Branch and Gristle set out for Mount Gloom. They wore backpacks to carry the salt in, though Gristle didn't see how Branch was going to carry much salt in such a tiny backpack. Since they were running out of time before the big picnic, Branch hoped the trip would go swiftly and smoothly.

It didn't start out that way.

"You know, you should probably ride on my shoulder," Gristle suggested.

"Why would I want to do that?" Branch asked.

The Bergen hesitated. He started to say "Because your little Troll legs are really short and dinky, so you're sure to slow us down," but he had a feeling Branch wouldn't react well to that. So instead he said, "Oh, I just thought it might work out better."

"How would it work out better?"

Gristle sighed. There seemed to be no way around just telling Branch the truth. "Because we'll go faster if I don't have to wait for you to catch up. Because your legs are, you know, a little shorter than mine."

Gristle was right. Branch did not react well.

"Oh, so you think my legs are too short, huh?" he said, bristling with anger.

Gristle shook his head rapidly. "Oh, no, no, no. It's not that. They're not *too* short. They're just . . . short."

"Actually," Branch said, trying to keep his cool, "the problem might be that *you'll* have trouble keeping up with *me*."

Gristle couldn't help snorting with laughter. "Me? Have trouble keeping up with a Troll? I seriously doubt—"

Before the king could finish his sentence, Branch whipped his long blue hair around his head three times and shot it forward. *WHAP!* It wrapped around the branch of a tree. Branch zipped forward! As he passed the branch, he unwrapped his hair and shot it toward a low branch on another tree. He used his long hair to swing from tree to tree, rapidly making his way through the woods.

"WHOOO-HOOOOO!" Branch whooped as he zoomed through the forest, propelled by his own hair power.

Gristle stared. "Huh," he said to himself. "I wonder if that's why they call him Branch." Then he realized if he stood there any longer, Branch would soon swing out of sight. "HEY, WAIT FOR ME!" He broke into a run, pumping his chubby arms and legs. "MY HAIR'S TOO SHORT TO DO THAT! ALSO, I DON'T KNOW HOW!"

With Branch swinging through the trees and Gristle running on his big Bergen legs, the pair made quick progress. But eventually their route to Mount Gloom took them through a dry patch of desert. There were no trees. And that meant no limbs for Branch to wrap his hair around.

Striding on his much longer legs, Gristle soon left Branch behind.

"HEY!" Branch yelled at the Bergen's back.

Gristle stopped and waited for Branch to catch up. "*Now* do you want to ride on my shoulder?" the king offered again, grinning.

Branch stubbornly shook his head. "No! I don't need a ride. I just need you to maybe . . . slow down a little."

Gristle shrugged. "Okay," he said. "But the big picnic will be here before you know it. And if we don't get back with the speckled savory salt in time . . ."

"I know!" Branch barked. "C'mon, let's go!"

Royal Cartographer. "Yup! It's called the Forest of Fetid Ferns!" He looked up at the woods as they drew nearer. "What's 'fetid' mean?"

"I think it means stinky," Branch said. As they reached the edge of the forest, he sniffed and made a face. "Yeah, now I'm *sure* it means stinky!"

CHAPTER SEVEN

Branch was absolutely right. "Fetid" means stinky. And the Forest of Fetid Ferns stank.

It *really* stank. It was just about the worst stink Branch and Gristle had ever smelled. They covered their noses with their hands, but the odor somehow slipped right through their fingers. They tried pinching their nostrils closed, but that didn't work, either.

"Do we *have* to go through the Forest of Fetid Ferns?" Branch asked. "This is *horrible*!"

Gristle looked at the map again. "Looks like it's pretty much the only route to Mount Gloom unless we want to go way, way out of our way."

"Right now I'd like to go way, way away from here!" Branch said. "I'm not sure how much more of this stink I can take!"

Gristle quickened his pace. "I'll try to get us through here as fast as I can. In the meantime, maybe we can pinch our noses with clothespins."

"Did you bring clothespins?" Branch asked.

"No," Gristle admitted. "Did you?"

"No," Branch said. "I didn't think we'd be doing laundry on this journey."

"Neither did I," Gristle said gloomily. "Man, I know we already said it, but I just have to say it again: THIS PLACE REALLY STINKS!"

Branch agreed. He took his vest off and tied it around his nose, trying to block the smell of the ferns. Then he buried his face in the soft fur of Gristle's cape.

Nothing worked.

But then something incredible happened. It started to snow!

"Snow?" Branch said. "But it's summer!"

"Who cares?" Gristle said, laughing. "At least this snow will cover the stink of the ferns!"

He was right. As the big flakes drifted down, the smell of the forest grew weaker and weaker, until they barely noticed it at all.

"I wonder why it's snowing at this time of year," Gristle said as he tramped along, happily kicking snow.

"I think we've been gradually climbing higher and higher ever since we entered the desert," Branch said. "At this elevation, it can snow even in summer!"

"Yeah, that's what I figured," Gristle fibbed.

Gristle began huffing and puffing, putting more effort into every step. The snow fell faster and faster—until it became a blizzard! The wind blew the snow straight into their faces. Gristle leaned into the gale, pressing through the swirling flakes. Branch shivered, trying to stay warm in the cape's thick fur.

Then the snowfall thickened and began falling so fast, it felt as though someone were dumping buckets of snow right on their heads. Gristle had to use his arms to plow through the deep drifts, digging a tunnel as he went.

"You know," he gasped, "I'm kinda starting to miss the stink."

"I have an idea," Branch said, tired of just riding along without actually doing anything. "You rest a minute in this clearing. There are trees here. I'll swing ahead a ways and try to see how much farther we have to go before we reach Mount Gloom."

Gristle looked doubtful. "These trees are covered in snow. Are you sure you can swing through them?"

"Absolutely!" Branch said. "Of course I can swing through them! In fact, with the branches slippery from the snow, I'll be able to move from tree to tree even faster!" Though he wanted to reassure the king, Branch actually wasn't at all sure he could swing through trees covered in snow. The truth was he'd never tried it before. He liked to spend snowy days snug in his underground bunker, warming his toes by the fire.

After picking out a branch that looked just the right height, Branch swung his hair around his head and shot it forward. *FWOOMP!* His hair slipped off the bark, knocking down a pile of snow, which fell on his head.

He shook himself off. "Just, uh, testing the slipperiness."

"Seems pretty slippery," Gristle said.

"Yeah," Branch agreed. "This time I'll take that into account. Okay, here goes."

He whipped his blue hair around in the air several times to make sure it was going really fast, then shot it toward the branch. *WHAP!* His hair wrapped around and held! Branch zipped past the tree, unwrapped his hair, and aimed it at the next tree. He was off, swinging through the snowy woods.

"Hurry back!" Gristle called.

As Branch made his way through the forest, he slipped and fell to the ground several times. But he was making good progress. After a few minutes, the trees started to thin out. He could see beyond the edge of the woods. And then he spotted it.

Mount Gloom.

It rose from the edge of the forest into the clouds—a steep, dark mountain covered with ice and snow. Branch shuddered.

But he'd found it. And that meant they'd soon be up in the crystal cave, collecting the speckled savory salt. Then they could go home!

He turned and hurried back through the woods, using his long hair to swing from branch to branch. During his solo trip out, the snow had seemed to let up a little.

But as he made his way back to the spot where he'd left Gristle to rest, the snow began to fall thick and fast again, coming down even more heavily than before. Huge wet flakes slapped his face as he swept through the trees. *FWAP! FWAP! FWAP!*

The branches were covered with so much snow, he could no longer grab them with his hair. He kept slipping and falling to the ground. Eventually, he gave up on swinging and just walked, trudging across the top of the tightly packed snow.

Luckily, he didn't have much farther to go. Branch recognized a tree leaning against a big red rock. He was almost there! He started to run, though it was slippery on top of the snow.

"Gristle!" he shouted. "I saw it! I saw Mount Gloom!"

He broke into the small clearing where he'd left Gristle.

No Gristle.

Where was the Bergen? Had he given up and gone home?

"GRISTLE!" Branch yelled as loudly as he could. "WHERE ARE YOU?"

Silence.

CHAPTER
EIGHT

Branch looked around frantically. He saw no
Bergen tracks in the fresh snow. That could
mean only one of two things. Either Gristle had
left so long before that his footprints had filled
with snow, or . . .

He was still here.

But where?

Branch scanned the ground, looking closer at

the blinding white snow. At first, it just looked like a smooth, blank sheet of paper.

But then he spotted something.

The tip of a gold crown was just barely sticking out of the snow. Branch ran to the crown and started digging frantically, calling, "Gristle! Gristle, are you okay?"

Soon he'd uncovered the crown and saw that it was still sitting on the Bergen king's flat green hair. Branch grabbed the hair and tried pulling. Deep in the snow, he heard a muffled "Ouch!"

There was no way Branch could pull Gristle out of the snow by his hair. But then he got an idea. Instead of using his small hands to dig with, he pointed his head toward the hole he'd started. Then he whipped his hair around and around Gristle, blowing the snow up and out of the deepening hole. *WHOOSH!* In no time, Gristle was standing in a hole in the snow that was slightly deeper than he was tall.

"Branch!" he called, wiping snow off his face. "You saved me!"

"Can you climb out?" Branch asked.

"I think so," Gristle said. "Let's see!"

Gristle reached up and managed to pull himself out of the hole, scrambling over the edge and flopping onto the packed snow near Branch.

"Whew!" Gristle gasped. "I must have fallen asleep. The snow fell so fast, I was buried! Thank you, Branch! You saved me!"

"Don't mention it," Branch said. "Come on! I saw Mount Gloom! It's not far!"

The snow had finally let up, so they were able

to quickly make their way out of the Forest of Fetid Ferns. When they reached the base of the mountain, they paused for a moment, looking toward the summit.

"It's a long way to the top," Gristle said, sounding worried.

"If Chef could climb up there, so can we," Branch said determinedly.

"Maybe there's a nice stairway," Gristle said hopefully. "With a red carpet."

"I kind of doubt it," said Branch. "But we can try to find a path."

The two of them explored the bottom of the mountain, hoping to find a smooth, clear path to the crystal cave. Gristle was hoping there'd be a friendly sign saying THIS WAY TO THE CRYSTAL CAVE!

But they found no sign. And they couldn't go all the way around the base of the mountain searching for the best path. The mountain was just too big, and they didn't have that much time.

Gristle grew frustrated. As a king, he was used to having things done for him. He'd already trudged through woods, a desert, and a bunch of stinky ferns. He'd even been buried in snow! He felt like he'd done enough.

"I think maybe I'll wait here," Gristle said. "I can, um, guard the base of the mountain to make sure no one follows you."

Branch looked confused. "Who's going to follow me?"

"Oh, you know," Gristle said vaguely. "Followers. Sneaks. Thieves. Bandits." As he said these things, Gristle started to change his mind. He didn't really want to stay alone only to be set upon by bandits and robbers! They might tie him up and steal his cape! Or his crown! "On second thought, I'll come with you."

He looked around desperately. "DOES ANYONE KNOW HOW TO GET TO THE CRYSTAL CAVE?" No one answered. All he heard was his own voice echoing off the rocks. *"CAVE . . . cave . . . cave . . ."*

"Don't think there are too many guides around Mount Gloom," Branch said. "Come on. This little path will have to do."

Branch started up a narrow path blocked in spots by rocks and slick patches of ice. It was tough going. It was so steep in places, they had to crawl on all fours, pulling themselves up by whatever handholds they could find. In other spots, they had to squeeze through narrow passages between huge boulders. This was fairly easy for Branch, but Gristle had to turn sideways and force himself through.

"Oof!" he said after a particularly tight squeeze. "Good thing I've been dieting!"

Several times they thought they were near the top of Mount Gloom only to learn they'd been fooled. They would pull themselves up over a ledge and think they'd reached the summit, but then see that the mountain went up and up and up.

"If this mountain were in my kingdom," Gristle grunted, pulling himself onto yet another rock shelf, "I'd have it lowered! It's WAY too high!"

"And just how would you go about having a mountain lowered?" Branch asked. "Command it to shrink?"

Gristle leaned forward and dug his feet into the side of the mountain as he climbed. "I'd leave the details to the experts," he explained. "As king, first you order the experts to come to you: 'Bring me the mountain-lowering experts!' Then you tell the experts to get to work. If they ask you how they're supposed to do the thing you've asked them to do, you just say, 'You're the experts! Do your best job! Now GO!'"

"Must be nice to be king," Branch said.

"Oh, it is," Gristle said. "Very nice. But it can get a little dull, sitting on the throne all day. That's why I agreed to come along on this shopping expedition instead of sending someone to do it for me. I thought it might be interesting to get out and see a bit of the world." He caught himself as he slipped on a stone. "I think next time I'll let someone else go."

They climbed in silence for a while, breathing hard, concentrating on where they put their feet. Most of the mountain was icy and slippery, so they had to keep their eyes peeled for good footholds. Neither of them wanted to tumble to the bottom.

Gristle was ahead of Branch, a little farther up the side of the steep mountain. "What's that?" he suddenly asked.

"What's what?" Branch said.

"There's a dark space in the side of the rock up ahead. Could it be the cave?"

"Do you see any crystals?"

"No, but it looks like—"

BLOOOOSH! Water shot out of a hole—and when it hit the cold air, it froze solid!

"Must be some kind of geyser!" Branch said.

Gristle hurried to the frozen column and rapped on it with his knuckles. *TINK! TINK!* "It's like a giant icicle! Only instead of hanging down, it's sticking up!" He climbed farther. "I wonder if there are any more—"

BLOOOOOOSH! Another geyser shot a thick column of water into the air—with Gristle on top of it! The water froze, and the Bergen was left standing on the icy column high above the side of the mountain!

Branch squinted at him. "What are you doing up there?"

"Nothing!" Gristle yelled back. "I'm just

standing! And wondering how to get down!" He peered over the side of the tower of ice. It was *way* too far to jump.

Branch looked up at the frozen geyser. It was too big for Gristle to wrap his arms around, but he got an idea. "Take your cape off!" he shouted to the king. "You can wrap it around the column. Hold on to both ends and slide down!"

Gristle raised his eyebrows. "Really? You think that'll work?"

"Pretend I'm one of your experts!" Branch called up. "Just try it!"

"Okay. Here goes!"

Branch watched Gristle unclasp his fur cape. He knelt at the top of the frozen waterspout and, holding both ends of the cape, swung it like a jump rope and hooked it around the column.

"Okay, now slide! Simple!" Branch shouted, trying to sound like it was no big deal to slip down a giant tower of frozen water jutting from a mountain. "It'll be fun!"

"If it's so fun, YOU do it!" Gristle yelled. He took a deep breath and stepped off the top of the geyser, quickly wrapping his legs around it. He started out screaming "WHEEE!" but almost instantly changed to "WHAAAAUUUGH!" He zoomed down the column of ice, reaching the bottom with a loud *THUMP!* He stood up and rubbed his rear end. "Not fun," he groaned. "Really not fun at all."

"Um, just curious. When you were up on top of the frozen geyser, did you happen to see the crystal cave?" Branch asked.

Gristle stared at the Troll. "No, Branch, I did

not see the crystal cave. I wasn't sightseeing—I was concentrating on getting down from a giant column of ice. Sorry about that."

"No problem," Branch said, heading up the mountain. "We'll find it when we find it!"

They hadn't gone much farther when they discovered that they'd climbed so high, they were inside a cloud. It was like being in a thick fog. Branch could still hear Gristle's feet on the slippery rocks ahead of him, but he couldn't see the Bergen at all.

"How are we ever going to find the crystal cave in this thick cloud?" Gristle wailed.

Branch was thinking the same thing. Had they climbed all this way only to get lost?

But then, as they trudged along the icy path, they finally broke through the top of the gray cloud. The sun shone. And above them, something sparkled.

"Is that . . . a crystal?" Branch asked.

"The cave!" Gristle said happily.

They hurried toward the crystal cave.

Then came a horrible, earsplitting screech. *CA-SCRAWW!* They looked up and saw a gigantic bird with a long hooked beak flying straight toward them, its sharp talons extended.

"THE WING-DINGLE!" Gristle screamed.

CHAPTER NINE

Branch and Gristle dove for the ground, slamming into the rock just as the wing-dingle swooped over their heads. It flew up into the sky, preparing to dive-bomb them again.

"I TOLD you the wing-dingle was real!" Gristle hissed at Branch.

"Okay, so it's real," Branch admitted. "How are we going to get past it and into the cave?"

"I have no idea," Gristle said. "BUT HERE IT COMES!"

The huge bird plummeted right at them, screeching. *SCRAAAW!* They crawled under rocks and hid, covering their ears. The wing-dingle soared up again.

Branch whispered to Gristle, talking fast. "Okay, here's what we're going to do. I'll distract the wing-dingle, and you make a run for it. Get in that cave!"

Gristle looked confused. "How are you going to distra—"

Branch had already jumped up and was running across the side of the mountain. "HEY, WING-DINGLE! LOOK AT ME! I MAY BE TINY, BUT I'M DELICIOUS!"

CA-SCRAWWWW! Screeching, the wing-dingle circled around, ready to grab Branch with its talons.

Gristle jumped to his feet and scrambled across the icy rocks, slipping and sliding, making his way toward the mouth of the crystal cave.

Branch stayed out in the open, waving his arms and jumping up and down. "WHOO-HOO, WACKY WING-DINGLE! CATCH ME IF YOU CAN, YOU BIG BIRDBRAIN!"

The wing-dingle dove, screaming down out of the sky, heading straight toward Branch.

Gristle slipped into the cave.

SCRAWWWW! Branch saw sunlight glint off the enormous bird's razor-sharp talons as it zeroed in on him.

At the last moment, Branch dove under a

rock he'd spotted earlier, barely squeezing into the tight space between the stone and the earth.

CRACK! The wing-dingle slammed into the ice that Branch had been standing on a split second before. Stunned, the bird managed to flap its wings and rise into the cold air, slowly flying away.

As the wing-dingle headed off, Branch dashed toward the cave, sprinting from rock to rock until he was safely inside. "Gristle!" he whispered. "Where are you?"

"Over here!"

Branch followed the Bergen's voice, running deeper into the cave. He found King Gristle crouched behind a large pink crystal.

"That was amazing!" Gristle said admiringly. "So brave!"

"Thanks," Branch said modestly. "Any sign of the speckled savory salt?"

Gristle shook his head. "Nope. I was hoping there'd be some kind of shop or something."

"You were thinking that inside this cave at the top of Mount Gloom, guarded by a ferocious wing-dingle, there'd be a nice little shop? Maybe with a clerk? And a tea counter?"

"I didn't say 'thinking.' I said 'hoping.'"

"Come on," Branch said, shaking his head in disbelief. "Let's look around."

They walked deeper into the cave. Light reflected off the facets of the huge, colorful crystals that lined the walls and ceiling. Every color imaginable was represented—from rose to purple to blue to yellow to orange to green.

"It's beautiful," Gristle whispered.

"Yeah," Branch agreed. "But where's the salt?"

"In the spice section?"

"I don't see any sections, or aisles, or shelves," Branch said, secretly rolling his eyes. "It's a cave, not a store."

They kept searching. Everywhere they looked, they saw big crystals that were each just one color. Until Branch looked down a long tunnel and spotted . . . speckles!

"Look!" he cried, pointing into the narrow tunnel. "Speckles! That must be the speckled savory salt!"

"Hurray!" Gristle cheered.

There was no way any Bergen could fit in the tunnel, so it was up to the Troll.

"Chef must have brought some kind of long

tool with her," Branch said. He went into the tunnel, scraped as much salt as he could carry into his small backpack, and came up to pass the salt to Gristle. He made several trips. He wished he had a shovel and a wheelbarrow, but they would have been hard to carry all the way up Mount Gloom.

"It's going to take a lot of salt to make all that pizza for the picnic!" Gristle said, filling his backpack. "Keep going!"

Finally, their backpacks were full of speckled savory salt. They headed past the colorful crystals and out of the cave.

"You know, I feel like we're forgetting something," Branch said as they walked into the sunlight.

"What could we possibly have forgotten?"

Gristle asked, picking his way across the icy stones. "We've got the speckled savory salt, and that's all we came for."

Suddenly, a huge black shadow passed over them.

"THE WING-DINGLE!" Branch yelled.

"Oh, right," Gristle said. "That!"

CHAPTER TEN

Without thinking, Branch and Gristle turned and ran back toward the crystal cave. But before they reached the safety of its chambers and tunnels, the wing-dingle swept down and grabbed Branch, tangling its talons in his thick blue hair!

"HELP!" he screamed as the huge bird started to fly away.

"OH, NO, YOU DON'T!" Gristle roared at the wing-dingle. Reaching up, he grabbed Branch's feet with both hands and held on tight.

The wing-dingle was a big, strong, ferocious bird, but even with its powerful wings, it wasn't able to lift Branch *and* Gristle off the ground and carry them away. The bird flapped its wings and strained, trying to pull the Troll out of the Bergen's grasp.

But Gristle didn't let Branch's feet go. Branch felt like a piece of dough stretched out before being twisted into a cinnamon roll. "AAAAGH!" he cried.

"LET GO, YOU MEAN OLD WING-DINGLE!" Gristle shouted.

But instead of letting go, the wing-dingle tried to peck at the king's face with its enormous beak. Gristle ducked, keeping his head just out of the bird's reach. "STOP IT!" he yelled. "I DON'T LIKE THAT!"

CA-CAAAW! the wing-dingle screeched. Gristle longed to cover his ears, but he didn't dare let go of Branch's feet.

"I wish I had something to shoo it away with!" Gristle yelled. "Even a stick would be good, but I don't see any up here! Maybe a rock . . ."

"Your crown!" Branch shouted.

"Crownie? Brilliant idea!" Gristle said. He quickly switched both of Branch's feet to his left hand, snatched off his crown with his right, and swung the crown at the wing-dingle. *SMACK!*

"Ooh! I bopped it!" cried Gristle.

SKWAAAAA! the wing-dingle shrieked. It

shook Branch from its talons and flew away! Gristle collapsed to the ground, still holding Branch. They were breathing hard.

"There," Branch gasped. "*You* saved *me*. Now we're even!"

Gristle put his crown back on and grinned. "Yeah," he agreed. "Even. Now let's get out of here before the wing-dingle comes back."

"I've got an idea for how to get down the mountain quickly," Branch said, looking at the steep expanse that lay below them. "Follow my lead!"

Branch took off his backpack and tossed it on an icy patch of smooth rock. Then he jumped onto his backpack and started snowboarding down Mount Gloom!

"Come on, let's go!" he called over his

shoulder as he sped down the snowy peak.

"I don't know . . . ," Gristle said, hesitating.

CA-CAAAW!

Hearing the screech of the returning wing-dingle, Gristle peeled off his backpack, tossed it down, leapt onto it, and sped down the mountain after Branch. "WHOOO-HOOOO!" he cried.

Lucky for Branch and Gristle, it was still snowy in the Forest of Fetid Ferns, so they didn't have to suffer through the horrible stench. Even better, they were able to ride their backpacks all the way through the frosty woods.

When they reached the desert, Branch didn't hesitate to let Gristle scoop him up and put him on his shoulder. Gristle ran through the barren country to the woods, where Branch used his hair to swoop through the trees. Before they knew it, they were right outside Troll Village.

And just in time.

The Bergens and the Trolls had already gathered in a beautiful clearing for the big picnic. Bergen stonemasons had built massive new ovens to cook the pizzas in. Woodsmen had found the perfect timber and stacked it in the ovens according to Chef's recipe. Under Captain Starfunkle's direction, cooks had mixed all the ingredients for the pizza in huge bowls.

All the ingredients, that is, except the speckled savory salt.

Captain Starfunkle was tapping his foot impatiently. "Where are they?" he asked. "We need that salt to finish the dough!"

One of the Bergen cooks pointed to the woods. "There!"

Gristle and Branch ran up, breathing hard and pulling off their backpacks. "We got it!" Gristle gasped. "We got the salt!"

"Oh, thank goodness!" Captain Starfunkle cried, taking the backpacks and handing them to his cooks. "Did the wing-dingle give you any trouble?"

Gristle and Branch looked at each other and grinned. "Nah," they said at the same time.

The cooks measured the salt, carefully following Chef's super-secret recipe. Then they mixed it into the dough, rolled the dough into balls, tossed the balls into the air to shape the crusts, placed the crusts on cooking stones, slathered on sauce and cheese, and popped the pizzas into the huge ovens.

"The pizzas are in the ovens!" Captain

Starfunkle announced. All the Bergens within earshot cheered, "HOORAY FOR PIZZA!"

At the Troll Village bakery, Biggie was running around frantically, directing the final loading and delivery of all the sweet baked goods. "There!" he said, sending Cooper off with a basket full of cupcakes. "That's the last of them!"

Smidge noticed a large bag in the corner. "What's in there?" she asked.

Biggie hurried over and peered into the bag. "Oh, no!" he cried. "These are the toppings for the big cookies I made! And those cookies have already gone to the picnic!" The big blue Troll was about to burst into tears.

"Don't worry, Biggie!" Guy Diamond said in his shimmery electronic voice. "We'll put these toppings on your cookies for you!"

"Yeah!" DJ Suki chimed in. "No problem!"

"Thanks, guys!" Biggie said, rushing out. "I'll see you at the picnic!"

"See you there!" DJ Suki said, waving. She turned to Guy Diamond and Smidge. "Okay, it's a pretty heavy bag, but I think if we all lift it together, we should be able to—"

But Smidge was already lifting the heavy bag by herself with her super-strong blue hair. "Got it," she said calmly, heading out the door. DJ Suki and Guy Diamond looked at each other, shrugged, and followed her out.

When they got to the picnic, they looked for Biggie's giant cookies. It was a busy scene. Trolls and Bergens rushed around carrying pastries, savory foods, drinks, and blankets.

"Where are the big cookies?" Guy Diamond asked.

"I don't know," DJ Suki said. "Can you two handle this? I've got to get the music started!"

"Sure!" Smidge said. "Go ahead and drop that beat!"

"Thanks," DJ Suki said, hurrying off to her Wooferbug.

Just then, a Bergen cook pointed to a batch of pizzas fresh from the stone ovens.

"These still need toppings," he told another cook.

"Got it," the other cook said.

"Did you hear that?" Guy Diamond asked Smidge.

"Yeah!" Smidge said. "Toppings! Those must be Biggie's big cookies! Come on!"

Over at the picnic site, everyone had finished spreading out blankets, and DJ Suki had started playing happy, bouncy music—perfect to picnic by.

"Hello, everyone!" Queen Poppy announced. "Welcome to the first-ever picnic for Bergens and Trolls . . . together!"

Everyone cheered. The Bergens were looking forward to tasting the famous pizza, and the Trolls were excited about all the pastries from Biggie's bakery. But the two groups weren't sure about each other's picnic offerings.

"See any hairs in their food?" one Bergen whispered to another.

"What *are* those?" one Troll whispered. "Marinated turnips? Who would eat THOSE?"

A line of Bergen chefs marched in, carrying

steaming-hot pizzas. A murmur of appreciation rose from the crowd of Bergens. The chefs set the pizzas down for all to admire.

"What's on those pizzas?" Branch asked quietly. "Are those . . . sprinkles?"

"Sprinkles?" Gristle hissed. "Pizzas aren't supposed to have sprinkles on them! Sprinkles are sweet, not savory!"

"Those are definitely sprinkles," Poppy whispered.

Sure enough, Guy Diamond and Smidge had mistakenly covered the pizzas with sweet sprinkles and toppings, thinking they were Biggie's big cookies.

"Oh, no," Gristle moaned. "This is terrible!"

"What's the matter?" Bridget asked him.

"Oh, nothing much," he answered miserably.

"Just that we're about to see protests, riots, looting, and the end of my reign as king of the Bergens!" He touched his gold crown. "Oh, Crownie, I'll miss you!"

Branch jumped to his feet. "Maybe we can stop them from serving those pizzas!"

But it was too late. The hungry Bergens were already crowding around the pizzas, eagerly grabbing slices and putting them on their plates. Actually, most of them didn't bother putting the slices on their plates. They bit straight into the pizza, burned the roofs of their mouths a little, chewed, swallowed, and said . . .

"DELICIOUS!"

The Bergens LOVED the sweet and savory pizza! And so did the Trolls! The combination turned out to be unbeatable!

The picnic was a huge success, thanks to the efforts of Branch, Gristle, and all the Bergens and Trolls who had worked so hard to make it happen. Every bit of the food was happily devoured— even the marinated turnips! And more than one Bergen found out that a little sweetness really made the savory tidbits even better.

King Gristle was thrilled. "We should definitely do this again next year!" he said later as they all watched beautiful fireworks lighting up the starry sky. "Or next month!"

"Definitely!" Poppy agreed. "From now on, the Troll-Bergen Picnic Fest-ganza-palooza will be a regular event!"

The others looked at her doubtfully.

"We'll keep working on the name," Branch promised.

THE END